By Laura French
Expanded by Diane Muldrow
Illustrated by Patti Gay

A GOLDEN BOOK • NEW YORK
Western Publishing Company, Inc., Racine, Wisconsin 53404

Library of Congress Catalog Card Number: 93-80012 ISBN: 0-307-30220-2 MCMXCVI

All over the world, people love cats.

Cats like Chester and Cookie and Sam are family pets. Like all cats—and just like people—they are alike in some ways and very different in others.

Chester likes to take naps on top of the TV set, where it's nice and warm.

Cookie knows where there's an open window at her house, so she comes and goes as she wants.

When Sam hears the alarm clock each morning, he runs to the bedroom to remind the people he lives with that it's time for breakfast.

Lions, tigers, leopards, and panthers are members of the cat family, too. They live in the wild.

All cats are excellent hunters. They move quickly and quietly on padded feet. Their sharp claws help them easily climb trees.

Cats hear especially well. Their ears, set high on their heads, can move in many directions to catch the faintest little sounds.

On a sunny day, the black pupil at the center of a cat's eye is just a tiny slit. But in the dark, the pupil gets bigger and bigger—to let in as much light as possible. That's why a cat can see so well in the dark.

The long whiskers on the sides of a cat's face are important, too—especially in the dark. They are "feelers" that tell the cat whether a space is wide enough for it to walk through.

Every cat has a coat of soft, warm fur. But the length and color of the coat help make each cat look different.

Most cats have short fur. But some cats, like the Persian, have long, thick, silky fur. Persians have snub noses, wide faces, broad chests, and short legs. They are quiet cats who seem to know that they are beautiful.

Siamese cats have long, thin faces and long legs. Their coats are usually light brown or fawn, but their feet, tails, ears, and faces can be dark brown, gray, or even orange or pale blue.

Siamese have loud, bossy voices, and they love to "talk" to people and to one another.

There are many other kinds of cats. Some of them are very unusual. The Manx cat is born without a tail—or with only a stump of one. The Rex cat has tightly curled fur—even its whiskers are kinky! Himalayans have long fur, like Persians—but they have white bodies and dark faces, tails, feet, and ears, like Siamese cats.

Of course, even the common kinds of cats are beautiful. Tabby cats have gray or orange fur that is striped or swirled. Tortoiseshell cats have coats of orange, black, and cream, all mixed together. Calico cats have spots of those same colors on a background of white.

Other cats have some special marking that's all their own—a black patch around one eye, a white stocking, or a little spot of color between the ears.

All cats are tiny and helpless when they are born. Their eyes and ears are tightly closed to protect them from bright lights and loud noises. They stay close to their mother, who feeds them and keeps them warm and clean and safe from harm.

After a few days, newborn kittens can hear, smell, and taste, but their eyes stay closed for up to ten days. When their eyes finally open, they begin to look around and play.

Their games of hide-and-seek teach them to hide from their enemies. By pouncing on a ball of yarn or chasing a piece of string, they learn to hunt.

By the time a kitten is six weeks old, it has learned to drink milk from a dish. At that time, it is old enough to leave its mother. And in less than a year, the kitten is able to take care of itself very well indeed.

People like cats because they are independent. That means that you can call a cat, but it won't come unless it wants to. You can pick a cat up, but it won't stay in your arms or on your lap unless it has decided that it's time for a nap.

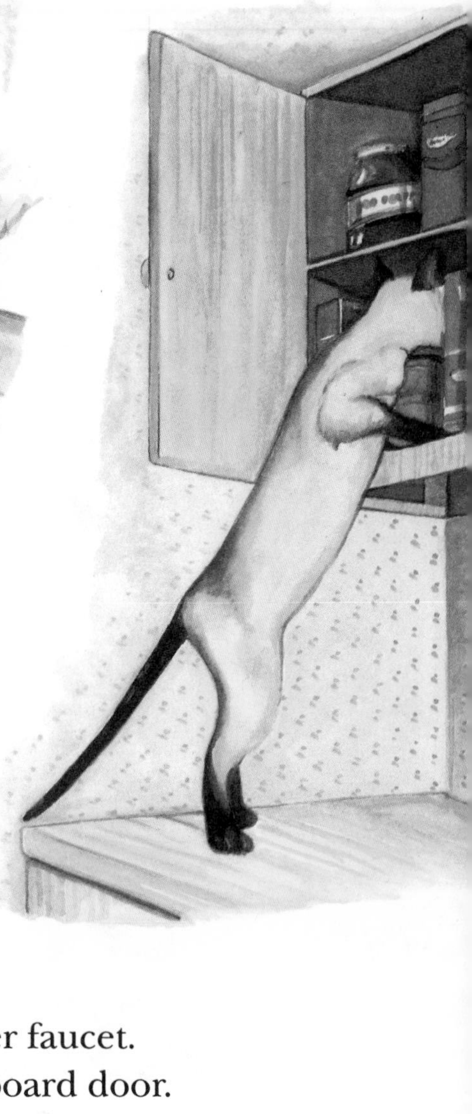

It's not easy to teach
a cat to do tricks, but if
a cat lives in your house,
it will learn tricks of its own.
Chester can turn on the water faucet.
Sam is able to open the cupboard door.

Cookie knows that there are good things to eat in the refrigerator, and she comes running when she hears someone open the door.

And every cat soon finds an especially comfortable place for stretching out to sleep.

Even though they are good at taking care of themselves, cats still need help from the people they live with. To be healthy and happy, they need to stay warm and dry. They need good food to eat and fresh water to drink.

If you take care of the cat who lives in your house, it will thank you in its own ways. It will greet you when you come home, stretching and yawning as it wakes from a sound sleep. It will sit close to you, purring and stretching its neck so that you can scratch that special place behind its ear or under its chin.

It will curl up at your feet when you settle down for the night. It will listen to secrets that you wouldn't tell anyone else.

The cat who lives in your house can be one of your very best friends.